I Can't Believe You SAID That!

BOYS TOWN
Press

Boys Town, Nebraska

Written by
Julia Cook

Illustrated by
Kelsey De Weerd

I Can't Believe You SAID That!
Text and Illustrations Copyright © 2014, by Father Flanagan's Boys' Home
(Book and Audio Book)
ISBN 978-1-934490-68-6

Published by the Boys Town Press
14100 Crawford St.
Boys Town, NE 68010

For a Boys Town Press catalog, call **1-800-282-6657**
or visit our website: **BoysTownPress.org**

Publisher's Cataloging-in-Publication Data

Cook, Julia, 1964-
I can't believe you said that! my story about using my social filter ... or not! / written by Julia Cook ;
illustrated by Kelsey De Weerd. -- Boys Town, NE : Boys Town Press, [2014]

   pages ; cm + Audio CD.
   (Best me I can be)

   ISBN: 978-1-9334490-68-6
   Includes book plus audio CD read by the author.
   Audience: grades K-6.
   Summary: RJ says what he thinks...no matter how it sounds or makes other feel. It's time RJ starts
using a social filter when he speaks. With help from his parents, he learns he doesn't have to verbal-
ize every thought that pops into his head. In fact, sometimes the less said the better.--Publisher.

   1. Children--Life skills guides--Juvenile fiction. 2. Thought and thinking--Juvenile fiction. 3. Oral
communication--Juvenile fiction. 4. Verbal behavior--Juvenile fiction. 5. Children's audiobooks.
6. [Conduct of life. 7. Interpersonal communication--Fiction. 8. Thought and thinking--Fiction.
9. Oral communication--Fiction. 10. Behavior--Fiction.] I. De Weerd, Kelsey, illustrator. II. Series:
Best me I can be (Boys Town)

PZ7.C76984 I133 2014
[E]--dc23   1409

Printed in the United States
10 9 8 7 6 5 4 3 2 1

Boys Town Press is the publishing division of Boys Town,
a national organization serving children and families.

My name is RJ.

Sometimes, I say things that get me into trouble
and I don't know why because I'm just being honest.

Last week, my dad and I picked my grandma up at the airport. On the way back to our house, I noticed how Spotted my grandma's hands and arms were, so I asked her, "Gram, how come your skin looks like a Dalmatian?"

"RJ!" my dad said. "I can't believe you just said that! That wasn't very nice! Apologize to Gram right now!"

"But, Dad, LOOK!"

"RJ."

"I'm Sorry, Gram."

A few days later, I was at the store with my mom. She was checking out, and I was standing over by the gumball machines.

"RJ, come and stand by me."

"No," I said.

"RJ, come over here by me now."

"I don't want to!" I said.

"RJ, over here NOW!"

"Mom, I don't want to stand by you! The lady next to you smells like she hasn't had a bath for a month! She stinks, Mom!"

"RJ!" my mom said. "I can't believe you just said that! That wasn't very nice! I think you owe this lady an apology!"

"But, MOM!"

"RJ."

"I'm sorry, ma'am."

On the way home, my mom told me that what I had said was rude. Then she told my dad about it and that night we had to have a talk in my room that lasted about 47 years.

Yesterday at school, Sam's mom
came into our classroom to help out.

"When is that baby in your tummy
going to be born?" I asked.

"RJ, I don't have a baby in my tummy," she said.

"Well then why are you getting **so fat?**"

9

"RJ!" my teacher said. "I can't believe you just said that! That wasn't very nice! Apologize to Sam's mom right now!"

"But, LOOK!" I said.

"RJ."

"I'm Sorry."

Then, I had to stay in from recess and write "I will not be rude to others" up on the board about a gazillion times!

Tonight, Blanche made her very first chocolate cake all by herself
and she wanted our family to eat it for dessert.
I think she left it in the oven way too long.

"I can tell you worked really hard on this, Blanche," my dad said.

"Pretty good for your very first cake," said my mom.

"I think it's nasty!" I said.

"It's burned to a crisp! It tastes like charcoal pie!"

Blanche started to cry, and I got in trouble.

"RJ!" my dad said. "I can't believe you just said that! That wasn't very nice! Apologize to Blanche right now and then go to your room!"

"But, Dad, LOOK!"

"RJ."

"I'm Sorry, Blanche."

After dinner was over, my parents came into my room to talk to me.

"RJ," my mom said. "You've really been saying rude things to people lately. You told Gram that her skin looked like a Dalmatian. You told the lady at the store that she smelled bad. Your teacher called and told me that you made a rude comment to Sam's mom. And tonight, you made Blanche feel terrible!"

"But I didn't lie," I said. "I told the truth! Grandma's skin has lots of spots, the lady at the store was stinky, Sam's mom is a lot fatter than she used to be, and Blanche's cake was nasty!"

"Besides, I was just giving them feedback. You always tell me that feedback is just information that helps you grow... so that's what I'm doing. I'm helping people grow."

"Feedback is a good thing, but you need to run your feedback words through your social filter before you let them come out of your mouth."

"My what???"

"Your social filter."

"RJ, you have two bubbles full of words in your head:
There's your THINKING bubble and your TALKING bubble.
These bubbles are connected by your social filter."

"When words form inside your head, they form inside your thinking bubble.
The words in your thinking bubble are private and only for you."

"When words come out of your mouth, they come from your talking bubble. The words that make it into your talking bubble are for everyone to hear."

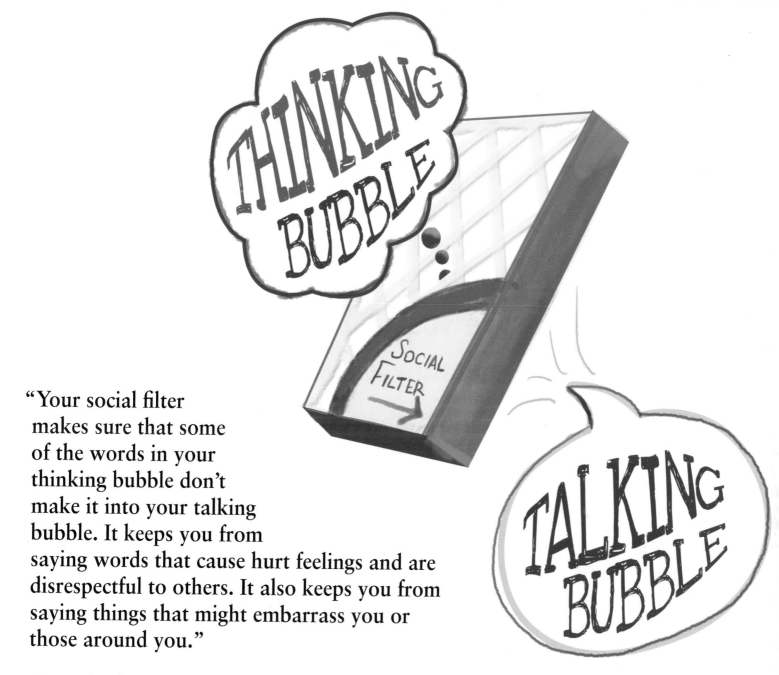

"Your social filter makes sure that some of the words in your thinking bubble don't make it into your talking bubble. It keeps you from saying words that cause hurt feelings and are disrespectful to others. It also keeps you from saying things that might embarrass you or those around you."

"RJ, I think sometimes you forget to turn your social filter on."

"You need to learn how to choose more appropriate words to say."

When you have something
that you want to say,
look at the situation
and the people around you.
Make sure you understand
the meaning of your words,
then think about who you will speak to.

Use your social filter to stop the words
that are mean, unkind or not right.
Then use the words that get through your filter.
And then you'll be alright.

"Like tonight when you made Blanche cry.
Inside your thinking bubble, you were thinking...

Blanche made a cake all by herself.

But the cake is really nasty
because she burned it.

I don't like the cake.

It tastes like charcoal pie.

But you should have filtered out the mean
words and said something like...

'It's really cool, Blanche, that you
made this cake all by yourself.'"

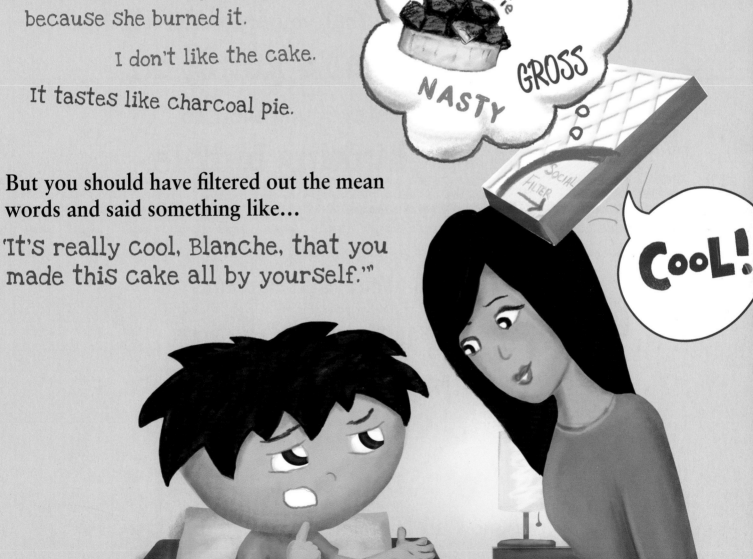

"And then, RJ," my dad said, "using your social filter can also keep you from saying things that will get you into trouble because it reminds you to analyze social situations."

"It reminds me to do what???"

Look at the people that you are around,
and figure out what's going on.
Think whatever you want to
inside your thinking bubble,
but make sure your filter is on.

Think about what happens
when you say the wrong thing.
Then filter through your thoughts.
Let your talking bubble
fill with respectful words,
and show all that you've been taught.

"RJ, if you can remember to keep your social filter turned on, your life will be SO much easier!"

I thought about everything my mom and dad said, and then I went to sleep.

Today at school, I used my social filter.

Bossy Bernice came to school with a brand new hair-do. She told everyone that her Great Aunt Betty had taken her to a hair stylist.

My thinking bubble filled up with:

Your hair looks really weird.

Your Great Aunt Betty must really nice if she wants to ha around you. I know I sure dor

It looks like the eagles have been nesting in your hair!

I used my social filter and only let some
of my words into my talking bubble, and then I said:

"Your great aunt
must be nice, Bernice."

Then later today,
I saw Norma the Booger Picker
stick her finger
all the way up her nose.

My thinking bubble
filled up with:

No, No, Norma!
Use a booger ghost!
And the words that
all of us always say...

Booger picker, booger picker
diggin' for a treat!
Norma picks her boogers;
and then she EATS!

I used my social filter, grabbed a box of tissues,
walked up to Norma and said:

"Hey Norma,
make a booger ghost, and use it
so you don't get teased."

My teacher heard me talking to Norma, smiled and said, "RJ, I can't believe you just said that!"

Then, a few minutes later, she handed me a Free Assignment Pass.

"I really liked your choice of words when you talked to Norma. Way to use your social filter!"

When I got home from school, Blanche told me that tonight,
     She gets to cook our whole entire dinner by herself.

My thinking bubble filled up with:

I'm going to starve!

Blanche doesn't cook... she burns!

She might set the house on fire!

I'll have to eat what she makes
and pretend that I like it, or
she will cry and I'll get in trouble.

Blanche is cooking all by herself.

Where's the **fire** extinguisher?

I used my social filter, and then I said:

"That's cool, Blanche!
Do you want me to be your assistant
so you don't have to do it all by yourself?"

"SURE!"

I can't believe
I just SAID that...
but it WORKED!

30

"I can't believe you just said that!" Sound familiar?

As humans, we have all experienced that awkward moment when another person thinks out loud and says or does something inappropriate. Teaching children to activate and effectively use their social filters can be a difficult process. Using your social filter effectively is a learned behavior. It demonstrates the ability to appraise a social situation and react or respond appropriately to that situation.

Here are a few helpful tips:

1. Explain the importance of using a social filter. Your social filter protects you from:
   - saying or doing things that are hurtful to others
   - saying or doing things that are hurtful to you
   - saying or doing things that might embarrass you
   - saying or doing things that might push others away and damage social relationships

2. Using pictures from the book, explain a concrete model of how a social filter works.

3. Role-play/discuss situations where a social filter is not used correctly and relationship damage is done.

4. Replay/discuss the same situations demonstrating what it looks like when the social filter is used correctly.

5. Model/discuss successful use of your own social filter daily for your child. Explain to your child often why you said what you said instead of what you thought, and what might have happened if you had chosen not to use your social filter.

6. Compliment your child for using his/her social filter effectively.
   - **Thinking Bubble:** This sweater that Grandma knitted for me is ugly and itchy and nerdy-looking. I will NEVER wear it!
   - **Talking Bubble:** "Grandma, thank you for making this for me… it must have taken you so much time!"

7. Explain to your child that there is a time and a place to VENT (say exactly what is on your mind). Make sure your child understands the WHERE, the WHO and the WHEN about venting.

For more parenting information, visit **parenting**.org

from BOYS TOWN.

31

Boys Town Press Books by Julia Cook

Kid-friendly books to teach social skills

COMMUNICATE with Confidence

A book series to help kids master the art of communicating.

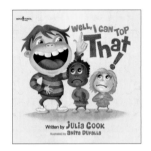
978-1-934490-57-0

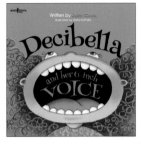
978-1-934490-58-7

Building RELATIONSHIPS

A book series to help kids get along.

978-1-934490-30-3

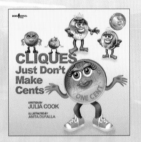
978-1-934490-39-6

978-1-934490-47-1

978-1-934490-48-8

978-1-934490-62-4

BEST ME I Can Be!

Reinforce the social skills RJ learns in each book by ordering its corresponding teacher's activity guide and skill posters.

MOM'S CHOICE AWARDS HONORING EXCELLENCE

978-1-934490-20-4
978-1-934490-34-1 (SPANISH)
978-1-934490-23-5 (ACTIVITY GUIDE)

978-1-934490-25-9
978-1-934490-53-2 (SPANISH)
978-1-934490-27-3 (ACTIVITY GUIDE)

978-1-934490-28-0
978-1-934490-32-7 (ACTIVITY GUIDE)

978-1-934490-35-8
978-1-934490-37-2 (ACTIVITY GUIDE)

978-1-934490-43-3
978-1-934490-45-7 (ACTIVITY GUIDE)

978-1-934490-49-5
978-1-934490-51-8 (ACTIVITY GUIDE)

978-1-934490-67-9
978-1-934490-69-3 (ACTIVITY

BOYS TOWN® Press

BoysTownPress.org

For information on Boys Town, its Education Model®, Common Sense Parenting®, and training programs:
boystowntraining.org | parenting.org
E-MAIL: training@BoysTown.org | PHONE: 1-800-545-5771

For parenting and educational books and other resources:
BoysTownPress.org
E-MAIL: btpress@BoysTown.org
PHONE: 1-800-282-6657